CRESTED BUTTE
FRIENDS
OF
THE
LIBRARY

P.O. BOX 791 • CRESTED BUTTE • CO 81224

Living in
Spain

Written by Su Kent

Photographed by David Hampton

SEA-TO-SEA
Mankato Collingwood London

This edition first published in 2007 by
Sea-to-Sea Publications
1980 Lookout Drive
North Mankato
Minnesota 56003

Printed in China

Library of Congress Cataloging-in-Publication Data
Kent, Su.
    Spain / by Su Kent
        p. cm. -- (Living in--)
    Includes index.
    ISBN-13: 978-1-59771-048-0
    1. Spain--Juvenile literature. 2. Spain--Social life and
customs--Juvenile literature. I.Title. II. Series.

DP17.K46 2006
943--dc22

                                                    2005058178

9 8 7 6 5 4 3 2

Published by arrangement with the Watts Publishing
Group Ltd, London

Series editor: Ruth Thomson
Series designer: Edward Kinsey
Additional photographs: Spanish Tourist Office pages 5(b), 8(l), 17(fl),
19(tr), 22(l), 23 (tr, br), 26(c), 27(t), 29(br); Catalonia Tourist Board
frontispiece, 9(c), 12(c), 13(tl), 28(r), 29(tl); Turgalicia 4(l); Carrefour 16(l);
Rachel Hamdi 9(r), 15(tr, br), 19(br); Neil Thomson 4(r), 8(c), 9(l), 10(l), 11(l),
14(c, r), 15(tc), 23(tc); Edward Kinsey 11(r), 16(c), 17(fl), 18(l),
20(l, cr), 26(l), 28(bl).

With thanks to Sarah Blyth

Contents

This is Spain

Spain is in southwestern Europe. It shares a peninsula with Portugal. The Pyrenees Mountains form a natural border with France. The northwestern coast faces the Atlantic Ocean. The south and east coasts face the Mediterranean Sea. The southern tip of Spain is only s short distance from North Africa.

△**Sierra Nevada**
These mountains, stretching across the south, include mainland Spain's highest peak, Mulhacén.

△**Northwestern coast**
Spain's coastline is more than 5,000 miles (8,000 km) long. The Atlantic coast is wilder than the Mediterranean coasts.

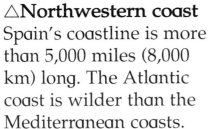

▷**The plains**
A hot, dry plateau (*meseta*) covers most of central Spain. Wheat and corn are the main crops grown here.

Fact Box
Capital: Madrid
Population: 40 million
National or official languages: Castilian Spanish, Basque, Galician, Catalan
Highest mountain: Mt. Teide, Tenerife (12,200 ft/3,718 m)
Biggest cities: Barcelona, Valencia, Seville, Alicante
Longest river: Tagus (626 miles/1,007 km)
Main religion: Roman Catholic
Currency: Euro

Atlantic Ocean

Bay of Biscay

FRANCE

Bilbao

BASQUE REGION

Pyrenees

Ebro River

CATALUNYA

Barcelona

Douro River

PORTUGAL

Guadarrama Mtns

Madrid

Tagus River

Valencia

Merida

Córdoba

Alicante

Seville

ANDALUCIA

Granada

Sierra Nevada

Mt. Mulhacén

Almeria

Menorca

Majorca

Ibiza

Formentera

Mediterranean Sea

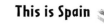

This is Spain

▷**Fishing**
Spain has the largest fishing fleet in Europe.

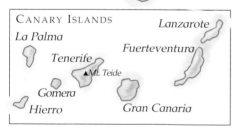

CANARY ISLANDS

La Palma

Tenerife

▲Mt. Teide

Gomera

Hierro

Lanzarote

Fuerteventura

Gran Canaria

▷**Volcanic islands**
The Canary Islands were created by volcanoes in the Atlantic Ocean, off the west coast of Africa.

Spanish islands

The islands of Majorca, Menorca, Ibiza, and Formentera in the Mediterranean Sea are also part of Spain, as well as the seven Canary Islands.

Madrid–the capital

In 1561, the Spanish king, Philip II, moved his court to Madrid, so that the capital was in the center of the country. It is more than 2,130 feet (650 m) above sea level and is the only European capital city without a river that big boats can use. One in ten Spaniards now live here.

A ticket and brochures about some famous sights in Madrid

△ *Grand Via*
This wide avenue cuts through Madrid. It is the commercial heart of the city, lined with banks, stores, offices, and movie theaters.

◁ **Royal Palace**
The Royal Palace, the Escorial, completed in 1764, has more rooms than any other European palace. It is used for state events by the present king, Juan Carlos I.

△ **The Prado Museum (*Museo del Prado*)**
The Prado houses Spain's oldest, finest art
collection. It includes paintings by many
famous Spanish artists, such as Velázquez,
Goya, and Murillo.

A thriving modern city

Madrid is the center of government,
industry, and banking. The major
industries are textiles, food, and metal-
working. The city also has several
museums of art, an opera house, a zoo,
an amusement park, and a bullring
with seats for more than 20,000 people.

▽▷**The *Retiro***
People come to
this large park
to walk, jog,
cycle, inline
skate, watch
puppet shows,
go boating,
or just to meet
their friends.

Famous sights

The Romans invaded Spain in 200 B.C. They called it *Hispania*, from which Spain takes its name. Ruins of Roman roads, ports, and viaducts can still be seen. North African Moors, who were Muslims, invaded Spain in A.D. 711. They built many mosques and palaces.

▷**Alhambra**
This Moorish fortified palace in Granada is famous for its great beauty. It is surrounded by red-brick walls that probably gave the palace its name—Alhambra means "red" in Arabic.

▽**Roman theater**
The Roman theater in Merida was built in 15 B.C. It can hold 6,000 people. It is still used for drama festivals.

◁**Córdoba** *Mezquita*
This mosque (*mezquita*) was built by the Moors. Later, Christian kings added two chapels and built a cathedral within the heart of the mosque.

Entrance tickets

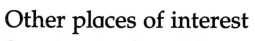

Other places of interest

Starting in the 15th century, Christians ruled the whole of Spain again and built many forts, cathedrals, and palaces. Some castles, monasteries, and palaces have now been converted into grand hotels, called *paradors.*

△Castles

Spain has more than 2,000 castles. Those near the southern coast were built against Moorish attack. Others were built as homes for wealthy nobles.

▷*Sagrada Familia*

Gaudí was Spain's most famous architect in the 20th century. His buildings include the *Sagrada Familia* church in Barcelona. This is still being constructed.

▽A movie set

The hot desert around Almeria, with its strange rock formations and dry riverbeds, is a popular location for making movies.

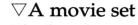

9

Life in cities

Just more than three-quarters of Spanish people live in towns and cities. With the exception of Madrid, all the main cities are found on the coast. In the center of every city there is a main square (*Plaza Mayor*), which people use as an everyday meeting place.

△**Seville Cathedral**
Grand churches, like this, were built after Spain discovered the Americas in the 16th century and brought back gold and riches.

▷ **Life outdoors**
On summer evenings, people gather in the town center to meet friends, go for a stroll, and relax.

△*Plaza Mayor*
The main squares are lined with bars and restaurants. A weekly market takes place in many of them. They may also be used for bullfights, pageants, and processions.

City development

In the past 40 years, most towns and cities have grown rapidly. People have moved there from the country to find jobs. Cities are ringed with modern apartments and shopping centers.

△▷Housing
In cities, most people live in apartments, often above stores. Some grow flowers on their balcony.

▽Fountains
The large, splashing fountains in many squares help cool the air on hot summer days.

△City tourism
Every town has a tourist office. This provides maps and guides for visitors.

Life on the coast

The sunny, sandy Mediterranean coasts (the *costas*) and the Balearic and Canary islands attract millions of people from all over Europe. Amazingly, there are more visitors to Spain every year than its entire population. Tourism provides many types of jobs for the Spanish.

△**Food and drink**
Some bars sell English and German food and drink for tourists.

▽**Seasonal jobs**
Hotels, restaurants, bars, and clubs provide seasonal work for one in ten Spaniards.

△**Beach vacations**
High-rise hotels and apartments line the beaches. More are being built every year.

▷**Coastal vacations**
Spaniards from inland head for the coast in August when the weather gets very hot.

▷**Fresh fish**
Fishermen provide fresh daily seafood catches for restaurants and hotels.

▽**Pottery store**
Spain is famous for its ceramics. Craftspeople make decorated tiles, pots, plates, and plant holders. Every region has its own style and designs.

△**Aquapark**
Some people work in recreation centers, like this one with water slides and swimming pools. They have been built in many resorts.

Tourist industries

Many small industries produce tourist souvenirs. These include handmade pottery, leather bags and belts, jewelry, lace, textiles, and baskets. These industries provide work for local people. Many of them are run by families.

Life in the country

Country life has changed dramatically over the past forty years as Spain has become more industrialized and tourism has grown rapidly. Today, one in ten Spaniards still work on the land, although many thousands of people have left the countryside to find work in cities or on the coast.

△**Village streets**
In hill villages, old houses line steep, narrow, cobbled streets.

△**Village people**
There are now more old people than young people in many villages. Small villages are often very isolated from one another.

◁**Changing villages**
New, detached houses have been built on the edge of villages within reach of large cities, either for commuters or as second homes. Old farms have been left to fall into ruins.

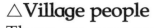

△Farming under plastic
Around Almeria, farmers grow vegetables and fruit in vast polythene greenhouses.
The crops often grow in a nutrient solution, instead of soil.

△Sunflowers
Sunflowers are grown for their seeds. These are pressed to make cooking oil.

△▷Olives
There are vast olive groves in Andalucia. Spain produces more olive oil than anywhere else in the world.

Olives

Olive oil

Farming

In the hot, dry south, farmers grow oranges, olives, grapes, avocados, and other fruit. In the cooler north, they grow cereal crops, herd cattle and sheep, and keep pigs.

▷Goats
Goats are bred for their milk, which is made into cheese (*queso*).

Shopping

In recent years, many supermarkets and hypermarkets have been built on the edge of towns. These sell lots of convenience foods for busy families. However, many people still shop for food at small grocery stores, specialty food stores, and daily (or weekly) markets near their homes.

△**A hypermarket**
Hypermarkets, furniture stores, and clothing stores are part of huge, new out-of-town retail outlets.

△**A covered market**
Most districts in cities have their own covered market (*mercado del barrio*). These sell fresh fruit, vegetables, meat, fish, bread, and cheese.

◁*El Corte Inglés*
There is a branch of the department store, *El Corte Inglés,* in every big city.

Butcher *(Carnicero)*

Fruit stand *(Fruteria)*

Fishmonger *(Pescadería)*

Bakery *(Panadero)*

△**Specialist shops**
People buy fresh food from specialist shops.

▷**Spanish produce**
These are some typical Spanish foods. They are exported around the world.

Almond cake

Smoked paprika

White tuna

Wine

Chorizo (Spicy sausage)

Pimentos

Sardines

On the move

Transport tickets

Only four out of ten Spanish households own a car—far fewer than in other European countries. Public transportation in towns and cities is efficient and cheap. Madrid, Barcelona, Valencia, and Bilbao have a subway (*metro*).

△▽Buses
Fares and tickets are the same for both buses and the *metro*. Some new buses in Madrid run on alternative ecofriendly fuels.

▷*The metro*
Madrid's *metro* is the third largest in the world. It has 202 stations and 11 lines that crisscross the city.

▷License plates
Until 2000, the first letters of a license plate showed where a car was registered. M was for Madrid and B was for Barcelona.

▷Fast trains

A high-speed AVE train connects Madrid with Seville. It travels up to 186 mph (300 km/h). The 260-mile (417-km) journey takes only two and a half hours.

△Commuter trains

Some trains have two decks to cope with the large number of commuters, who travel into the city for work every day.

▷Highways

Drivers pay to use some of the highways *(autopistas).*

▽Donkeys

In hilly areas, people still use donkeys to carry their crops home from the fields.

Trains and roads

Railroads and highways spread out from Madrid connecting with other large cities. A new highway runs along the south coast, easing heavy tourist traffic. In remote areas with little traffic, roads are poorly kept.

Family life

Most Spanish families are very close. They eat many meals together and, on weekends, visit grandparents or go for a stroll (*paseo*). In summer, families spend much of their time outside, having meals in cafes or restaurants with friends and relatives or playing sports.

◁▽Breakfast (*desayuno*)
Breakfast is usually a bowl of cereal, pastries, and a chocolate milk drink.

▽Evening meal
Families eat their evening meal together, often around 9p.m. Children go to bed after 10p.m.

Pastries

Coffee

Hot chocolate mixed with cereal

Toast and honey

◁**Homework**
Children have an hour of homework every night to prepare for frequent tests.

TV guide

Soccer cards

◁△**TV watching**
Popular programs include Spanish sitcoms and cartoons from North America and Japan. Children like *Megatrix*— a mixture of cartoons, activities, and games.

◁▷**Time to play**
Many boys collect soccer cards and play soccer in their nearest playground.

Time to eat

The Spanish use a great deal of olive oil, tomatoes, garlic, onions, and bell peppers in their cooking. Beef, pork, lamb, and seafood are eaten everywhere. Some meat dishes are made with fruit and almonds. This type of cooking was introduced to Spain by the Moors.

△Lunch
People eat their biggest meal of the day at lunch time (*comida*). Many restaurants serve lunch starting at 2p.m.

▷Cafes
Many people have a midmorning snack (*almorzar*). They often eat doughnut strips (*churros*) with a hot drink or juice.

△Menu of the day
By law, as part of their menu, restaurants have to offer an inexpensive, set-price meal. It includes two courses, dessert, bread, and a drink.

▽▷ *Tapas*

Tapas bars offer a huge variety of freshly cooked snacks, which people eat after work or between meals.

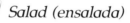

Olive oil and vinegar

Bread (pan)

Salad (ensalada)

△ *Gazpacho*

This cold tomato soup is a refreshing summer dish.

▽ *Paella*

Paella is a rice dish made with pork, chicken, fish, and shellfish. It is cooked in a large, shallow pan.

Meatballs (albondigas)

Squid (calamares)

Potatoes with a chili sauce (patates bravas)

Spicy sausage (chorizo)

Spanish omelette (tortilla)

School time

Children have to go to school from the age of six until 16. Most go to free state schools. Some go to private schools that charge fees. Many private schools are run by the Church, where pupils are taught by nuns and priests. All schools follow a national curriculum.

△**Going to school**
Most children go to a school near their home or to one near where their parents work.

▷**Lessons**
There are up to 25 pupils in a class. They learn reading, writing, math, art, and science. They begin English lessons at the age of seven.

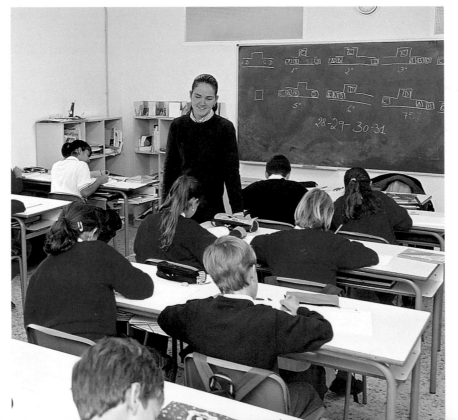

△**School hours**
Children go to school from Monday to Friday. Primary schools start at 9:30a.m. and end at 4:30p.m. There is a two-hour break for lunch.

▽Schoolbags

Every day, pupils bring the books they need for class in bags with wheels.

△Extra activities

After school, some children learn another language. Others do Spanish dancing, or judo. Many play soccer. In the summer, swimming in outdoor pools is popular.

▽Timetable

Private schools start earlier and finish later than state schools and have an hour for lunch.

Secondary schools

Pupils go to a secondary school at the age of 13. Some leave at 16 and take courses to learn a trade. Others stay on to study for the *bachillerato*, which they have to pass if they want to go to university.

Having fun

The Spanish like to spend time outdoors. In colder months, many of them ski, play ball games, or take daily strolls around town. In hot weather, they go swimming in local pools or at the beach. Some people go sailing or windsurfing.

△A lottery kiosk
The lottery is very popular. People buy tickets from kiosks run by blind people. The income helps pay for aids for the blind.

△Rollerskating
In cities, young people rollerskate in the parks. They also play volleyball, basketball, and soccer.

◁Skiing
People ski during winter weekends at ski resorts in the Sierra Nevada, the Pyrenees, or the Guadarrama mountains.

▽Bullfighting

Bullfights take place in the summer months. Skilled bullfighters *(matadors)* twist and turn to avoid the charge of fierce bulls.

◁*Pelota*

In the Basque region, players take turns hitting a hard rubber ball against a wall in a fast game called *pelota*.

Soccer badges for Real Madrid and F.C. Barcelona

Sports

The Spanish enjoy watching sports. Soccer is a national passion. Their teams are very successful—Real Madrid has won the European Champions League nine times. Bullfighting and *pelota* are sports that both began in Spain.

Celebrations

There are religious and folk festivals (*fiestas*) throughout the year in Spain. Sometimes, people dress up in the traditional costume of their region. They parade through the streets, dance, or perform feats of physical strength and daring.

▽Giants

In Barcelona, people parade giant figures through the streets. The figures dance stiffly to music in the main square.

▽A human pyramid

In the Catalunya region, village teams compete to create the highest human pyramid (*casteller*). When the lightest person reaches the top, he raises his arm in triumph.

◁Flower festival
In June, many towns hold competitions, where people create carpets of flowers in the street.

◁▷The Seville Fair (*Feria*)
During the week-long *feria* in Seville, men wear fitted black suits and women wear bright, layered *flamenco* dresses. They parade in carriages or on horseback and sing and dance.

Going further

Spanish products

Look around a supermarket for foods that have come from Spain. Spanish fruits will usually have a label with *España* on them. Can you find any oils and vinegars produced in Spain? What else can you find?

Design a poster

Make a poster to advertise a flamenco festival. Draw a colorful picture of women with flouncy dresses, head-dresses, and clicking castanets. Add a headline and details about the time and place of the event.

Create a carpet

Use the flower carpet competition as inspiration to make one of your own. Glue colorful paper scraps on to a piece of cardboard. You could either make a pattern or choose a typical Spanish image.

Websites

www.yahooligans.com/around_the_world/countries/spain
www.cybersleuth-kids.com/sleuth/Geography/Europe/Spain.index.htm
www.cyberspain.com

Glossary

Border The boundary that separates one country from another.

Commuter Someone who travels some distance from home to work each day.

Currency The money used in a country.

Export To send goods or produce from one country to sell in another.

Fertile Fertile land is good for growing crops.

Hypermarket A gigantic store that sells a wide range of products including food, clothing, and electrical goods.

Industry The making of goods, from raw materials, for example, making cloth from wool, cotton or nylon, usually in a factory.

Monastery A place where a community of monks live.

Mosque A Muslim place of worship.

Nutrient A chemical substance that helps plants to grow healthily.

Pageant An outdoor entertainment where people dress up in costumes and act out scenes from history.

Peninsula Land surrounded by water on three sides and joined on one side to a larger land mass.

Plain A large area of open flat land.

Plateau A flat highland.

Population The number of people who live in one particular place, such as a town or country.

Seasonal Describes something that is affected by or changes with the seasons.

Suburb The outer area of a town or city where many people live.

Viaduct A long, arched bridge that takes a road over a wide valley or river.

Volcano A cone-shaped mountain lying over an underground chamber of molten rock. Sometimes pressure from hot gases causes a volcano to erupt.

Index

Page numbers in *italics* refer to entries in the fact box, on the map, or in the glossary.